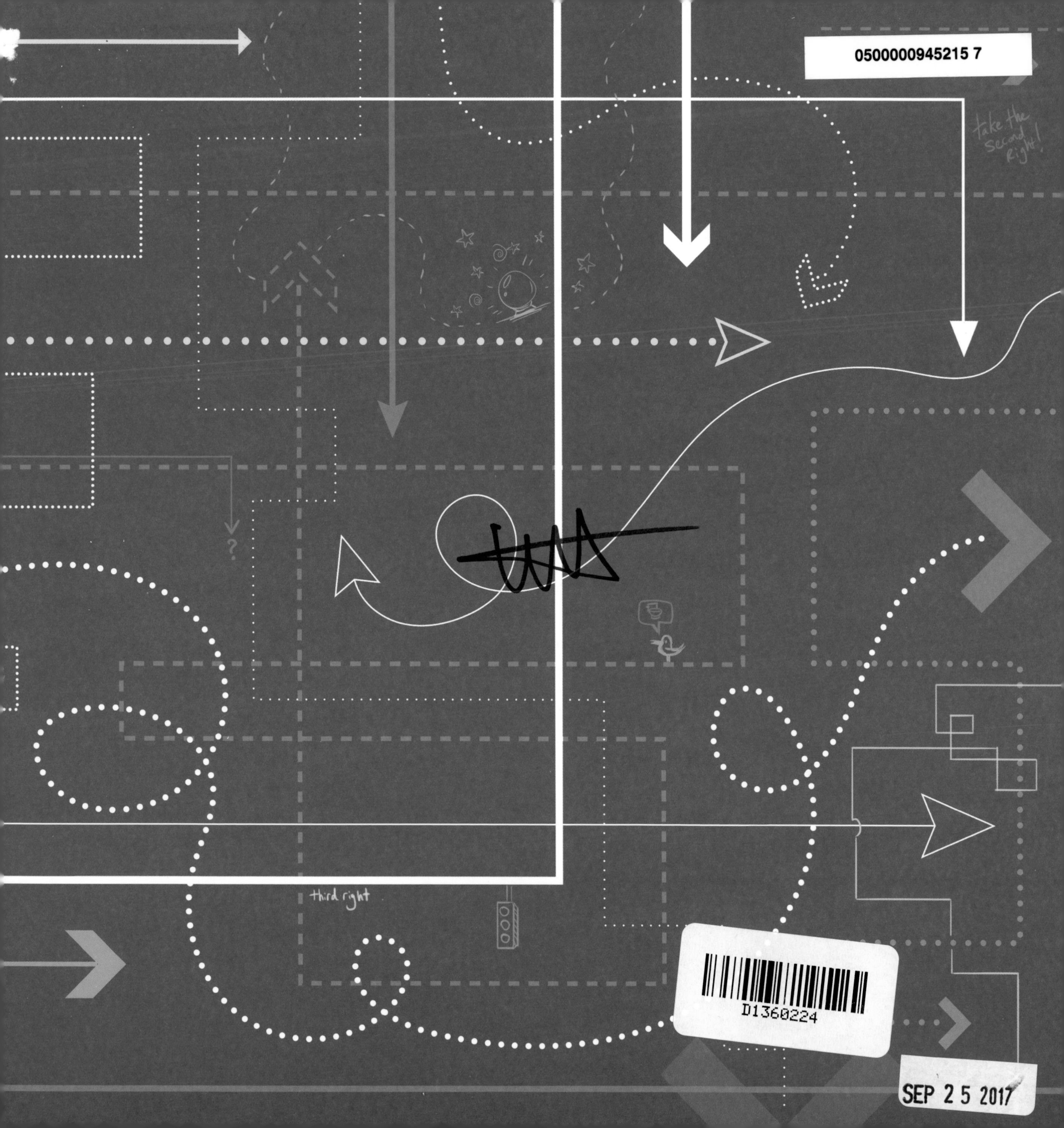
take the second right!
third right

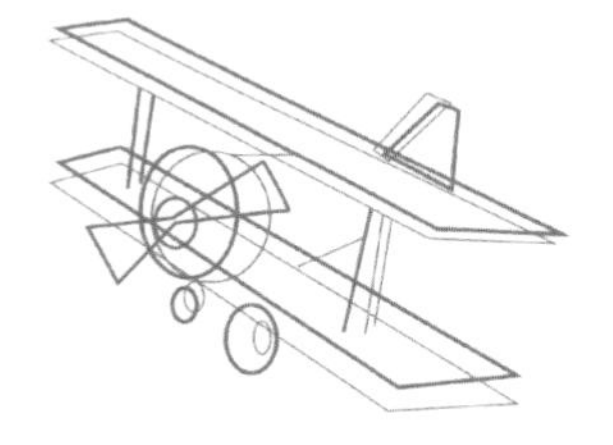

978-1-938700-40-8

Published by Commonwealth Editions, an imprint of Applewood Books, Inc.
P.O. Box 27, Carlisle, Massachusetts 01741

Visit us on the web at www.commonwealtheditions.com
Visit Shankman and O'Neill on the web at www.shankmanoneill.com

Printed in China

10 9 8 7 6 5 4 3 2 1

Commonwealth Editions
Carlisle, Massachusetts

I had to find the bathroom but I didn't know the way.
So I stopped and asked a waiter at the Morning Star Café.
Where's the bathroom, Mister, please?
I really need to know.
And I hope it isn't far
because I really have to go.

I'm glad you came to me, my friend.
I love to give directions!
If the bathroom's what you're looking for,
then here are my suggestions:

Go straight into that building with the statue of a **clown**.
Take the escalator **up** and take the elevator **down**.

You'll exit on the other side
and **walk** a block or so.
I'm sure they have a bathroom there,
and someone ought to know.

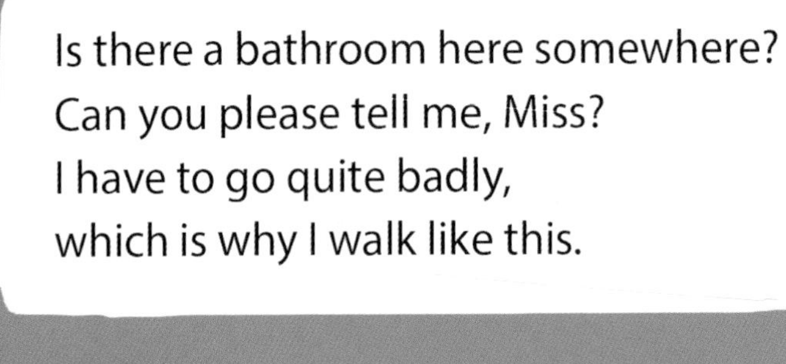

I've seen that walk a thousand times.
I know it well indeed.
And when you walk like that, young man,
a bathroom's what you need.

I know it must be **somewhere**
because that's where most things are.
And if you end up **nowhere**,
then you'll know you've gone too far.

In that case **turn around**, I think.
But don't turn all the way.
'Cause **spinning** round and round like that
could keep you there all day.

Go **south** when you feel **happy**.
Go **north** when you feel **blue**.
When you need a rest, it might be best
to stop and **tie your shoe**.

Then take the **brightest hallway**.
Go through the **biggest door**.
And ask whoever's there
if he or she can tell you more.

SOUTH
NORTH
PUSH
Can anybody help me, please? I need a bathroom soon.
I've needed one for quite some time—I've had to go since noon.
And how far is this bathroom? Did they put it on the moon?
I really have to go, you know, I feel like a balloon!
Have no fear,
an old man said,

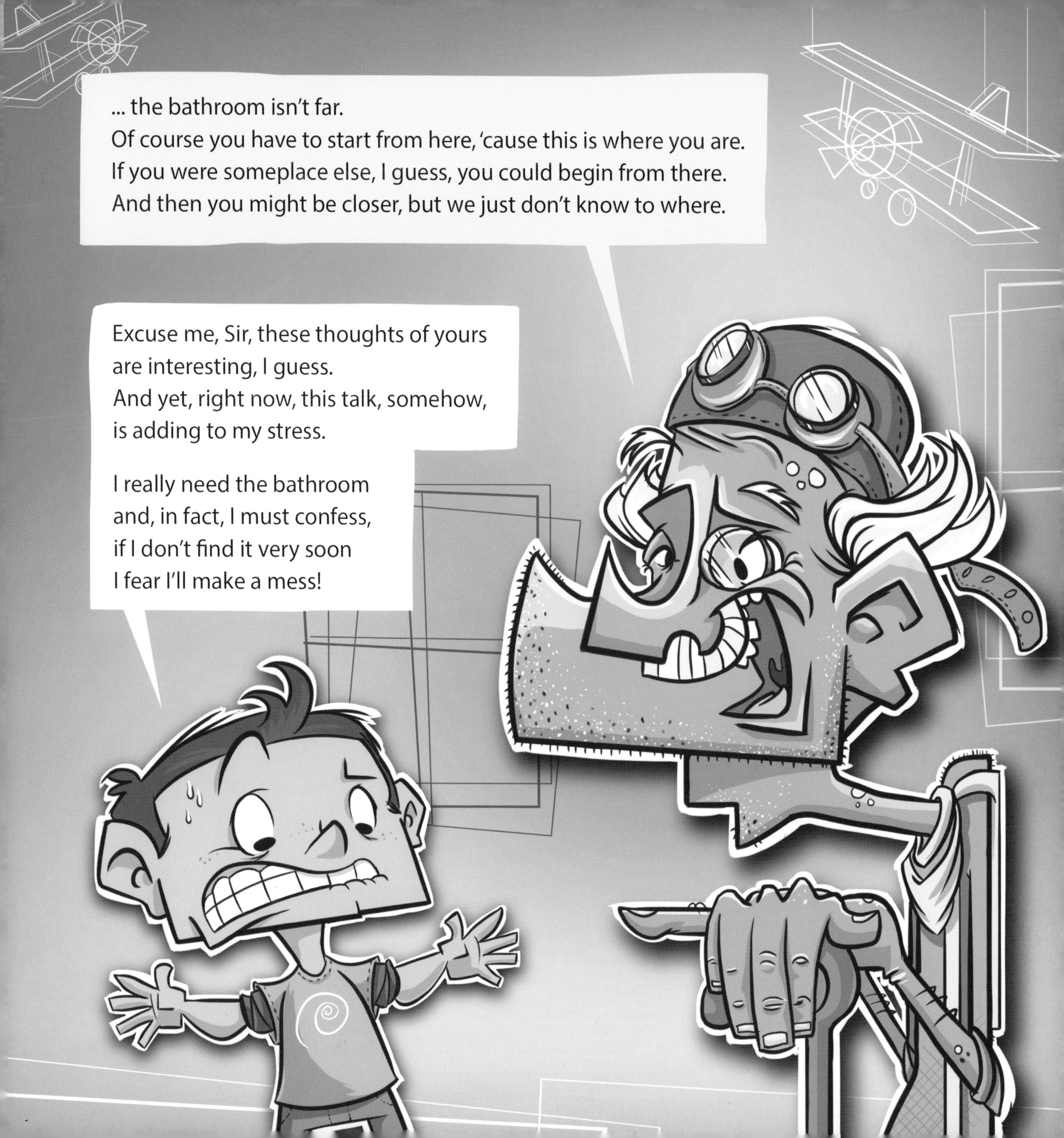
... the bathroom isn't far.
Of course you have to start from here, 'cause this is where you are.
If you were someplace else, I guess, you could begin from there.
And then you might be closer, but we just don't know to where.
Excuse me, Sir, these thoughts of yours
are interesting, I guess.
And yet, right now, this talk, somehow,
is adding to my stress.
I really need the bathroom
and, in fact, I must confess,
if I don't find it very soon
I fear I'll make a mess!

Well, why didn't you say so?
That's no problem in the least.
Just walk around the bend
and **take the 9 Bus going east.**

When you get off at the station
you can ask the **ice cream man.**
Just let him know I sent you
and he'll tell you if he can.

Hello. I need the bathroom
and I don't know what to do.
I asked the old man on the street
and he sent me to you.
A wise decision, I must say.
That old man's very clever.
He knows I use the bathroom.
I've been using it forever!
I started going first
when I was only three or four.
And that, of course, was long before
I owned the ice cream store.
You see, I wasn't sure I would
become an ice cream man.
It was that or being president.
I had to choose a plan.

Excuse me, Sir, that's very nice.
I'm sure I'd vote for you.
But first I need the bathroom.
Can you please give me a clue?

Am I close enough to see it?
Is it coming into view?
The reason that I'm asking
is the old man said you knew.
Of course I do, my friend,
and you're not very far at all.

I once went twice as far
to practice yoga at the mall.

I had to wear an outfit
that was very tight and small.

And I couldn't do the handstand
without leaning on the wall.

I'm sorry, Sir, I hate to interrupt a yoga master.

But isn't there some way
to help me find the bathroom faster?

I've heard that it's around here
and that you know where it is.

And I absolutely,
positively
have to take a whiz!

I understand the problem.
Do not say another word.
I know the way, I'm pleased to say,
exactly as you've heard.
Go **through the park** and **up the hill**
and **past the eagle's nest**.
The **lady with the parasol**
will tell you all the rest.

the lady said,

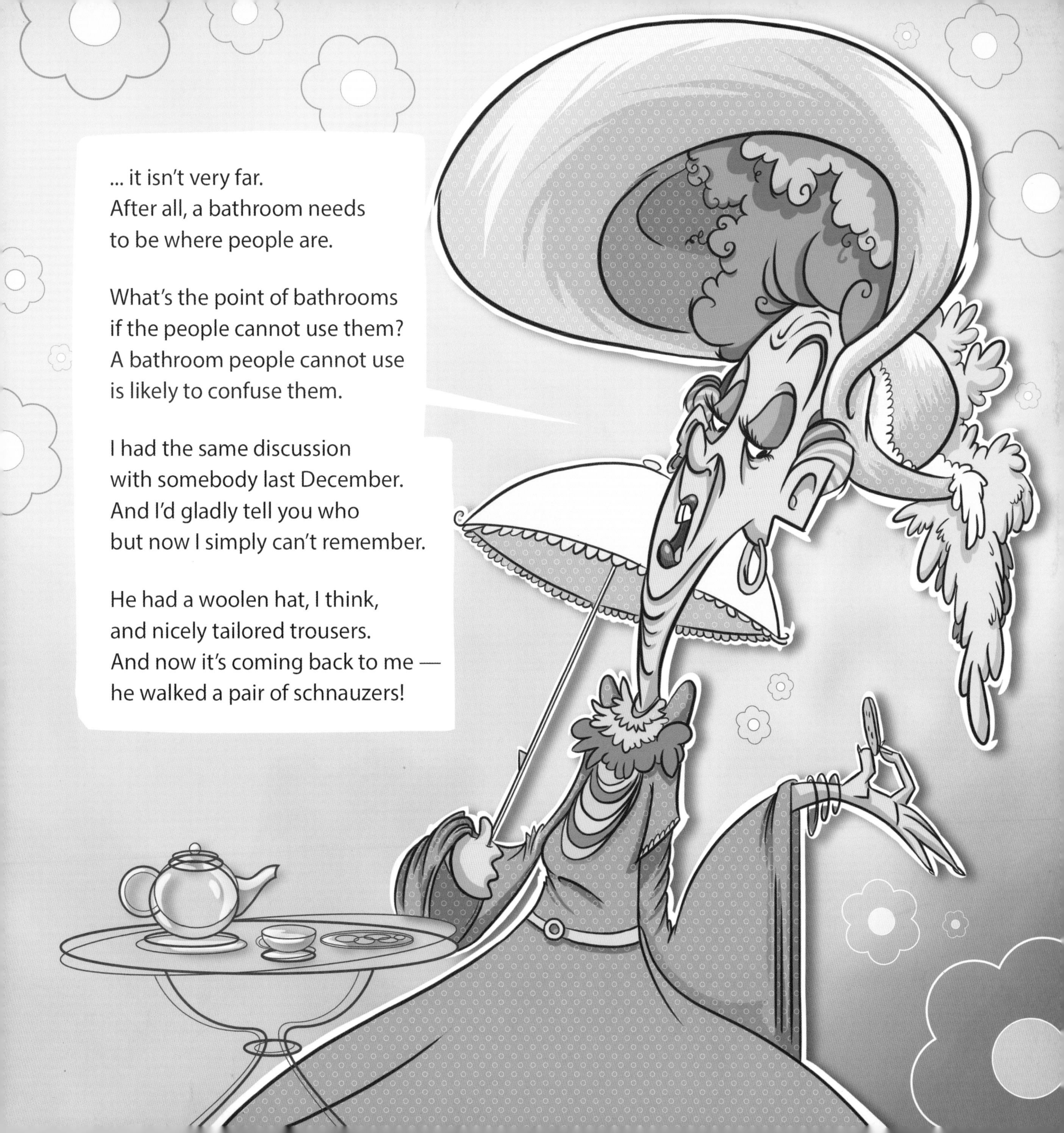
... it isn't very far.
After all, a bathroom needs
to be where people are.

What's the point of bathrooms
if the people cannot use them?
A bathroom people cannot use
is likely to confuse them.

I had the same discussion
with somebody last December.
And I'd gladly tell you who
but now I simply can't remember.

He had a woolen hat, I think,
and nicely tailored trousers.
And now it's coming back to me —
he walked a pair of schnauzers!

I'm glad you got your memory back. The pants sound very nice.
But if you wouldn't mind, I am in need of your advice.
As you know, I need to go — it could be any minute.
And the bathroom won't do any good ...
unless, of course, **I'm in it.**

Yes, yes, of course, I understand:
You really need to pee.
You might try **turning left or right**.
That's always worked for me.

And I have found that **walking faster**
moves the bathroom closer.
But if you still don't see it,
I suggest you ask the grocer.

Help me, please, I need to find the bathroom very fast.
I have to go and don't know how much longer I can last.
The lady with the parasol thought you'd have the directions.
She told me so herself between her many recollections.

Ah, yes, she likes to talk about
that fellow's tailored pants.
She talks about them every time
I give her half the chance.
The pants were not the least bit special,
from my point of view.
And I'd tell her so myself,
but then what good would that do?

Excuse me, Sir, I'm sure you have an expert's eye for fashion. As for me, I cannot say that clothing is my passion. Right now, in fact, I'm much more in a bathroom state of mind. So please direct me to it, Sir, if you would be so kind.
Right away, but you should know, that bathroom isn't much. A toilet here, a toilet there, a sink or two and such.

You'd think they'd put a picture up to add a touch of class.
A statue or a chandelier or maybe some stained glass.

Once again, it's clear
you have an eye for fine detail.

But it's getting to the point
where I'd be happy with a pail!

So point me to an IGLOO
or a CABIN
or a TEE PEE,

I DON'T NEED
A CHANDELIER, SIR ...

I JUST NEED TO MAKE A PEE PEE!

Well, why didn't you say so? I can send you right away!
Just mosey down the **dock** and float the **boat** across the bay.

S.S.P.P.

It's a short walk to the **train ...**
TRAIN:
300 MILES

... then grab a **taxi** to the **plane**.

And when you land you'll see a **tall blond lady walking a Great Dane**.

Just ask her where the bathroom is. She'll point you there, I'm sure.
After all, she is a friend of mine, and that's what friends are for.

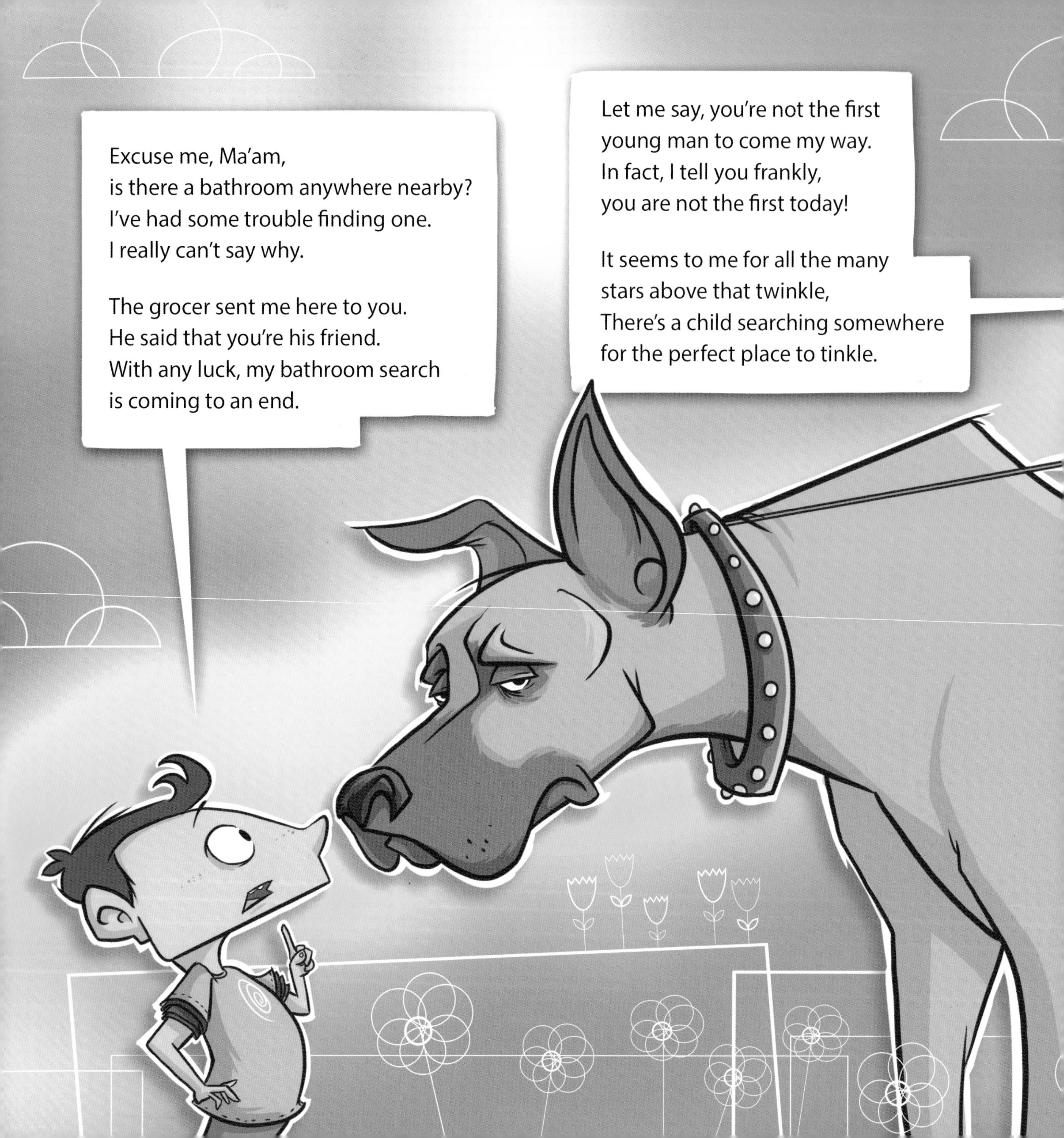
Excuse me, Ma'am,
is there a bathroom anywhere nearby?
I've had some trouble finding one.
I really can't say why.

The grocer sent me here to you.
He said that you're his friend.
With any luck, my bathroom search
is coming to an end.

Let me say, you're not the first
young man to come my way.
In fact, I tell you frankly,
you are not the first today!

It seems to me for all the many
stars above that twinkle,
There's a child searching somewhere
for the perfect place to tinkle.

Here's my advice to all of you
who seek and cannot find:
Instead of more directions,
try to change your state of mind.

I suggest you try to **smile**.
I suggest you **sing a song**.
If the notes are right I bet you'll find
your way before too long…

I can't believe my eyes — I see the bathroom door from here.
It's just a few more feet away. At last, I'm very near!
But wait a second, who's that man beyond the bathroom door.
He just looks so familiar. Have I seen that face before?

Of course, that's him, the waiter,
at the Morning Star Café,
the first one that I asked —
the one who sent me on my way.

But now I see, what he told me
was absolutely wrong.
The bathroom, it turns out,
WAS RIGHT BEHIND US ALL ALONG!

So I could blame the waiter or try to change the past.
But there's something better I can do ...

... and I'm doing it at last!
Aaaaaaaahhh

hhhhhhhhhh...
Loo
(whew)

ALSO by Ed Shankman and Dave O'Neill

The Sea Lion's Friend
When a Lobster Buys a Bathrobe
My Grandma Lives in Florida
The Boston Balloonies
The Cods of Cape Cod
I Met a Moose in Maine One Day
Champ and Me by the Maple Tree
The Bourbon Street Band Is Back

Also by Ed Shankman with Dave Frank

I Went to the Party in Kalamazoo

Ed Shankman

Ed Shankman's entire life has been one long creative project. He has been writing children's books since he himself was a child. He performed for many years as a lead guitar player and is an impassioned, if imperfect, painter. He has also published his novel, *The Backstage Man*, which was written over the course of three decades. And he has spent his professional career directing creative teams within the advertising industry. Today, Ed lives in New Jersey with his wife, Miriam, who is the love of his life, and their two cats.

Dave O'Neill

Dave O'Neill is an illustrator and art director. Throughout his career, Dave has worked with several advertising and marketing agencies, where he specialized in children's brands and experiential event planning. When he's not illustrating the various steps of the pee-pee dance, he moonlights with an improv comedy troupe and designs toys in his spare time. This is Dave's ninth book with Ed, and the duo agree that it's time for a movie studio to approach them about an *I Met a Moose* movie. Today, Dave is a husband to a cool girl and a father to a cool, smaller girl. More of Dave's work can be found on his art blog at oneilldave.blogspot.com.

www.shankmanoneill.com

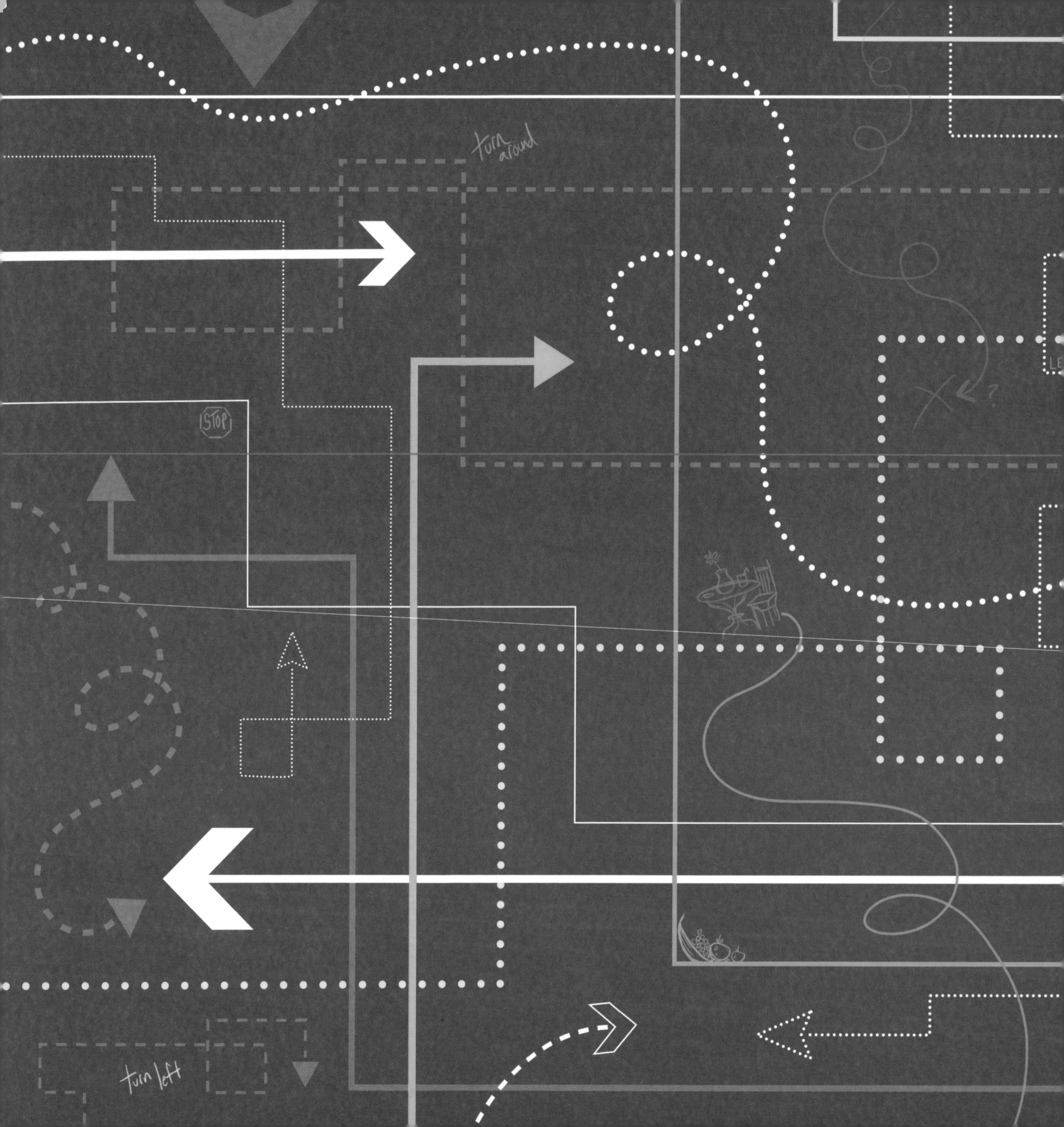
turn around
STOP
turn left

MyMarketingLab: Improves Student Engagement Before, During, and After Class

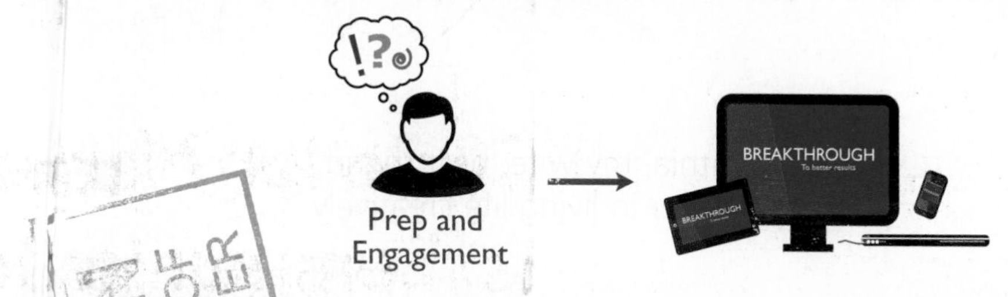

- **NEW! VIDEO LIBRARY** – Robust video library with over 100 new book-specific videos that include easy-to-assign assessments, the ability for instructors to add YouTube or other sources, the ability for students to upload video submissions, and the ability for polling and teamwork.
- **Decision-making simulations – NEW and improved feedback for students.** Place your students in the role of a key decision-maker! Simulations branch based on the decisions students make, providing a variation of scenario paths. Upon completion students receive a grade, as well as a detailed report of the choices and the associated consequences of those decisions.
- **Video exercises – UPDATED with new exercises.** Engaging videos that bring business concepts to life and explore business topics related to the theory students are learning in class. Quizzes then assess students' comprehension of the concepts covered in each video.
- **Learning Catalytics** – A "bring your own device" student engagement, assessment, and classroom intelligence system helps instructors analyze students' critical-thinking skills during lecture.
- **Dynamic Study Modules (DSMs) – UPDATED with additional questions.** Through adaptive learning, students get personalized guidance where and when they need it most, creating greater engagement, improving knowledge retention, and supporting subject-matter mastery. Also available on mobile devices.

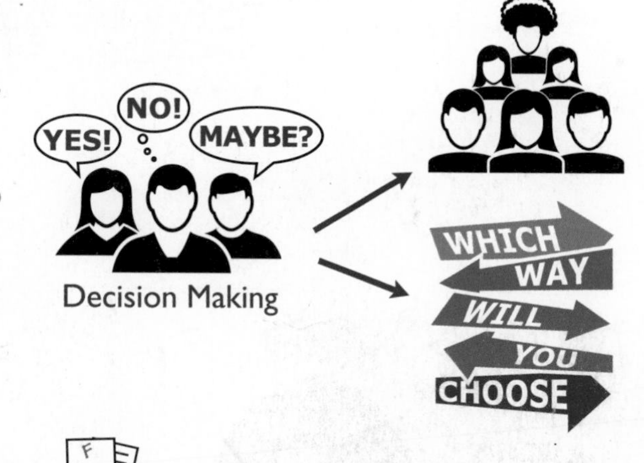

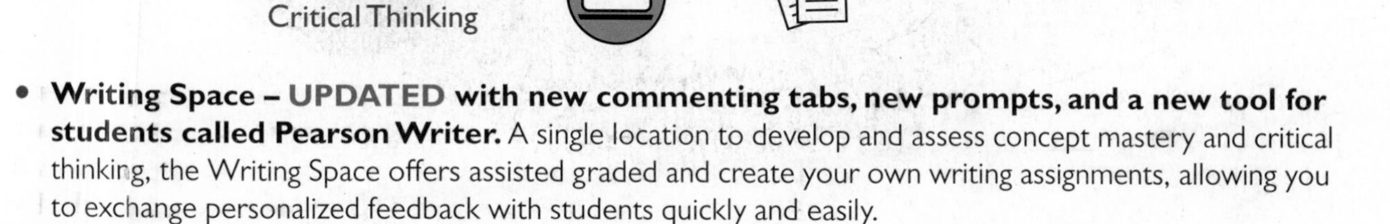

- **Writing Space – UPDATED with new commenting tabs, new prompts, and a new tool for students called Pearson Writer.** A single location to develop and assess concept mastery and critical thinking, the Writing Space offers assisted graded and create your own writing assignments, allowing you to exchange personalized feedback with students quickly and easily.

  Writing Space can also check students' work for improper citation or plagiarism by comparing it against the world's most accurate text comparison database available from **Turnitin**.

- **Additional Features** – Included with the MyLab are a powerful homework and test manager, robust gradebook tracking, Reporting Dashboard, comprehensive online course content, and easily scalable and shareable content.

http://www.pearsonmylabandmastering.com

PEARSON

To Cynthia, my wife, best friend,
and partner in living life creatively.

—WJK

In memoriam:
Warren J. Keegan 1936–2014

—MCG